VANQUISHING THE VIKING

BY

ANNABELLE WINTERS

Copyright Notice

Books by Annabelle Winters

The CURVES FOR SHEIKHS Series

The CURVES FOR SHIFTERS Series

The CURVY FOR HIM Series

The CEO and the Soldier
The Astronaut and the Alien
The Botanist and the Biker
The Psychic and the Senator

THE CURVY FOR THE HOLIDAYS SERIES
Taken on Thanksgiving
Captive for Christmas
Night Before New Year's
Vampire's Curvy Valentine
Flagged on the Fourth
Home for Halloween

THE CURVY FOR KEEPS SERIES
Summoned by the CEO
Given to the Groom
Traded to the Trucker
Punished by the Principal
Wifed by the Warlord

THE DRAGON'S CURVY MATE SERIES
Dragon's Curvy Assistant
Dragon's Curvy Banker
Dragon's Curvy Counselor
Dragon's Curvy Doctor
Dragon's Curvy Engineer
Dragon's Curvy Firefighter
Dragon's Curvy Gambler

THE CURVY IN COLLEGE SERIES
The Jock and the Genius
The Rockstar and the Recluse
The Dropout and the Debutante
The Player and the Princess
The Fratboy and the Feminist

WWW.ANNABELLEWINTERS.

VANQUISHING THE VIKING

BY

ANNABELLE WINTERS

1
ELEVENTH CENTURY A.D.
SOMEWHERE OFF THE COAST
OF ENGLAND
WENDRA

The acrid smoke from their fires still burns in my nostrils as the Viking longship races away from England's coastline towards the cold North Sea. I want to close my eyes to block the sight of my once-thriving village being turned to ash, but the sights inside my head are far worse than what I see on the shore. So I keep my eyes open and watch my village burn. I watch in silence as the cold wind blows my dark hair wild like battle flags, makes my brown skirts billow like bloodied sails.

The silence moves deeper into me as I strain at the leather straps binding me to the wooden mast near the ship's bow. My wrists already bleed from the rough rawhide, but it is no matter. Once we face the icy North winds of the open sea, I will feel no pain. The cold will take me slow and sweet like a lullaby. Death will come like a dream.

"Perhaps then I will see that all of this is a dream," I whisper, my dry lips cracking as I smile. "A dream in which all those who fell in battle today will rise again, go back to their families, kiss their wives, hold their children."

A horn sounds from one of the other Viking longships, breaking me out of my dream. I turn my head towards the sound just as the ship pulls up alongside and keeps pace. Even through my hatred for the invaders I cannot help but admire their skills on the sea. The longships themselves are works of wonder—vessels large enough to traverse the open oceans but light enough to sail shallow waterways like rivers and creeks for raids that come silent and swift.

"Swiftly now," comes a man's deep voice from behind me. I try to look at him but my neck will not turn that far without breaking. "Overtake us so the captives can see her. See their queen."

A chill that comes not from the wind goes through my back, and my jaw tightens as I see the women and children of my village on their knees on the open decks of the second ship. Behind them stand lines of Viking warriors in chain-mail armor and helmets of shining steel. They carry battle-axes and broadswords, wear beards and beads, sport hair long and wild. Their faces are stained with the blood of my warriors, and I get some small satisfaction when I see that some of them bleed from wounds that I pray will kill them slow and painful. May they die whimpering in their beds like children instead of on the battlefield like men.

"The males of your tribe are on the third longship," comes the man's voice, this time much closer. Still I cannot see him, but when the wind dies I smell him.

His scent is unlike that of any man I have known, and I will never forget it. Even if I never see his face I will hunt him by that scent of whale-oil and leather, salty sweat and metallic blood. But there is something else in his musk that strikes me, and I sniff the air again and frown. It is a pungent, masculine oil but not one that I know. An earthy aroma that steadies my heart but confuses my mind. Why does a monstrous marauder douse his body with oils? Could it be his natural scent? Why does it affect me so?

His words confuse me too. I assumed the Vikings would kill all the able-bodied men like it has been rumored. They do not take slaves, I have heard. They do not kill the very young or the very old, instead leaving them behind. But I saw children and the elderly on the longship that passed us. And if what this Viking says is true, that the surviving men of my tribe are on the third boat, then it is very strange indeed. Vikings do not act thus.

The man's scent draws near, and the sun moves from behind a cloud and shows me his shadow on the salt-weathered wood of the foredeck. His size and shape startles me, and I blink twice and swallow once as I wonder if he is some kind of man-beast, a creature with the body of a bull and the head of a man.

"Do I not speak your tongue well enough?" he says, his shadow stiffening, his chain-armor clinking as he takes a step toward me and stops. "Do you not understand my words?"

"I do not understand your actions," I say calmly even though my heart flutters like the canvas sails high on the mast above me. "What will you do with the children and the old? What will you do with my warriors?"

"They are no longer your warriors, Queen," says the man, still in shadow like he knows that staying hidden gives him a subtle power over me. I understand power very well, and that is why my heart flutters: Because this Viking understands it too. Why else would he call me Queen? "They live because I allow it, which means they belong to me now."

My thick thighs tighten beneath my skirts, and I wet my cracked lips and hold my tongue. He stays silent too. I wait, but the only sound is that of the sleek ship cutting through the cold waves. His shadow remains steady even through the ship's motion, like he controls the tides and currents just like he does his ships and soldiers.

Just like he does me.

"You call me Queen," I say finally. "England already has a king and queen. I have no crown. I wear no fine silks. No precious stones adorn my body."

No response. Then a short laugh. "Crowns and jewels are borne by thieves and fools as often as they are by kings and queens," he says. His shadow moves. "You revealed yourself with character, not a crown, Lady Queen."

"How so?" I ask.

"You were the only woman who showed no fear," he says as he finally steps forth and turns to face me. He stands taller than his shadow revealed, broader than any bull I have seen, with heavy muscles that appear sculpted with great care and deadly precision. He is more handsome than I care to admit, with strong cheekbones and wise eyes that simmer green like molten emeralds. His jaw is brutally masculine but his speech is measured and refined. He looks into my eyes unflinchingly, and I shudder as he lets his gaze roll down along my curves, past my high-buttoned blue tunic that the wind blows tight against my breasts, down to where my brown skirts hug my wide hips. "You showed no fear," he says again, the edges of his eyes crinkling with the hint of a smile. "Even though you felt it."

I blink and my breath catches. "You are mistaken," I say stiffly. "I felt no fear then. I feel no fear now. All you can give me is pain, and I have lived through more pain than you can understand. All you can take from me is my life, and that is not so precious as you might think."

He tilts his head and studies my face. He runs a hand along his jutted jaw and grunts. "More pain than I can understand? What do you know of what I can and cannot understand?"

"Maybe nothing," I say. "Maybe everything."

He laughs with his eyes and his mouth and his shoulders. "Now I *know* you are a Queen," he says, stepping back and crossing his thick arms over his chest. His face settles into a smile, and his eyes do something to my heart I do not understand . . . do not *want* to understand. The smile does not stay long, however, and when the man looks past me towards the north, his gaze narrows and a shadow passes behind those eyes. His throat moves as he swallows, and then he turns from me and stares at nothing.

The second ship has passed us, and the third longship overtakes us. I see my warriors bloodied but alive on the decks, their eyes turned toward me. I show no expression, yield no emotion. I worry not for my warriors. They are ready to die and if that is their fate they will welcome it. And though I do worry for the children and the old, the strange truth is they are better off here than left behind in the ashes of a burned village. I am glad of it. In our village we respect our elders, rely on them to teach the young, to preserve our ways. Our tribe is part of England but also not. We did not lose a war to the Crown and we are not foolish enough to think we would win independence with a few hundred fight-

ers. But we are far from the towns of the kingdom
and our way of life is as it was before England had
a king or queen or castles or even a name.

"What is your name?" I ask the man, swallow-
ing my pride and yielding to the truth that we are
prisoners and this man appears to be the leader
of the Viking raiders. He speaks our tongue and
he carries himself with what could be called grace.
But of course the Vikings are said to be savages,
and so again I am confused. I burn to know more
about him. The more I know, the better my posi-
tion. My warriors failed to defend the tribe. Now
it is up to me.

The man strolls past me and shows me his back.
He wears no helmet and although his hair ap-
peared wild at first, on closer inspection he is more
groomed than I would expect. In fact many of the
Vikings appear to care for their hair and skin and
even their nails. Some wear beads around their
necks and colorful ropes around their wrists.

"Wolruff," he says, his head half turned and looking bigger than the masthead on the longship's bow.
"What are you called, Queen?"

"Wendra," I say, my heart pulling as Wolruff turns
to me and shows a smile that hides emotion I cannot understand, just like I cannot understand why
my heart pulls. We look at each other as the third

longship moves ahead. The seas are empty and open, the water a blue steel-gray. The wind has slowed but yet the sails pull hard and strong.

He glances toward the other two ships ahead and then looks at me. From his brown leather belt he pulls a long dagger with a jeweled hilt and a blade of polished steel. I swallow as he draws close, and when he circles around the mast to which I am bound and grasps my hands, I gasp out loud as the contact moves heat through my body.

Wolruff cuts the rope with a single stroke, and I collapse in a heap of skirts at the suddenness of being released. He grasps my arm and pulls me to my feet, and I lean against him as my head spins. There must have been strain I did not measure, stress on my body and perhaps my mind. My cheeks burn red with shame at my weakness, and I firm my jaw and move away from his support.

"You hide your fear well," he whispers when I grasp the mast as the ship hits a swell. "But the body can only hold up so long. Come. There is salted meat and brown ale below decks. You need it, and so do I."

He turns but stops when I do not follow.

"Your tribe will be fed. I have seen to it," he says through that knowing smile. "Come."

He moves toward me but stops again when I

flinch. I am wary of going below decks. The rumors of Viking men have reached every female ear on England's coast. They are as brutal in the bedroom as on the battlefield, say the whispers. They take many wives and lovers, discarding them like an Englishman might discard his old boots. If that is Wolruff's intention, then let him show it above decks, in full view of the sea and sky, the gods and goddesses.

"Fear not, Wendra," he says, smiling but not looking into my eyes. "You will not be touched." Abruptly the smile dies and his eyes narrow and his jaw tightens. "Not by me, at least."

Then he turns and storms below decks, leaving me with those words, words that chill me even as what I saw in his eyes warms me. I glance towards the open water, blinking as I ponder throwing myself over the side. Perhaps I will grow a tail and turn into a mermaid. Perhaps my body will wash up on an island and I will be reborn as a siren, drawing Viking sailors to their deaths with my sweet song.

The thoughts bring a smile to my lips. I watch the coast of England disappear over the horizon, glance at the cold waters once more, and then turn towards the dark arched doorway that leads to the bowels of the longship.

You will not be touched, he'd said. *Not by me, at least*.

2

WOLRUFF

The thought of someone else touching her makes my body burn with rage that not even a battle can inspire. But I cannot keep her. I may be Captain of my fleet and Commander of my Raiders, but in the North I must bow to my King. Bow to him and pay tribute.

The tribute of a Queen.

"Your Queen will not eat and she will not drink," comes the voice of Carab, my First Mate. He stands outside the open door to my chambers, and from his speech I know he has drowned himself in brown ale along with the rest of the men.

I turn and look at him. He is a good man but something about his tone does not sit right. I rub my beard and click my jaw. It is the way he said *Queen*. I referred to her as a Queen and the men laughed, I remember now. She wears dull brown skirts and a tunic fit for a fisherwoman, one of them had drunkenly said with a raised wooden mug of ale, but Wolruff thinks he has captured the Queen of England!

The men had roared and rocked, and I had grinned wide and raised my own mug. The men fight for me and they will die for me, but I do not ask them to bow to me. I am no king. I do not lust for power the way King Nordwin does. I chase the thrill of adventure, the joy of battle, the delight of plunder. I care not for the particular spoils or trea-sure—only the act of taking.

I suppose that is a form of power-lust too, I think as I nod at Carab so he knows I am on my way out to the food hall. When I enter the wood-walled hall I see Wendra seated with a straight back and closed eyes on a bench at the Captain's table. My table. Men sit at the other tables drinking ale and chewing salted dried herring, bones and all. There are some chuckles and whispers, but even those die down when I enter.

"Clear the hall," I say quietly, my attention on Wendra. I do not care if she eats or not. The jour-ney across the North Sea is short and she will not starve. Besides, if she wanted to take her own life, she had the chance when I left her alone above decks. She could have rolled over the railing and ended it. Instead she chose to face her fate in this life and not the next.

The word *fate* rings in my head like wedding bells, and I bite my lower lip and fight back the possessive fury that makes me want to keep her as mine. Already my mind churns like a storm-sea, tossing up ways to deny King Nordwin his tribute without incurring the small man's famously big wrath. Nordwin won his throne by equal measures force and cunning, and although he is civil to those who show loyalty, he does not tolerate insult or disobedience.

And denying Nordwin his tribute would be both.

The room empties noisily, and I wait for stillness to fall. When it does I silently watch Wendra. She is calm like a goddess at the altar, and her energy does something to my heart and my cock all at once. I want to plunder her treasure on the Captain's table, push my bearded face under her skirts and sniff her like a hound. My nose twitches and my hair stands on end when I imagine what her cunt will smell like, what her slit will taste like, how her big buttocks will feel in my meaty paws. And then the rage rises again as I imagine Nordwin violating those curves and making her his . . . until the next Viking Raider brings him the next tribute.

It has never bothered me before, I think as I cross my arms over my chest and take long, slow breaths. I watch her shoulders and breasts move as she breathes, and again my heart does that thing and my cock does that other thing. Her washed-out blue tunic fits her perfectly, and I make out the faint protrusion of her nipples. They are big like saucers, and I lick my lips and fight back a wild urge to claim her now. I could lie to Nordwin and present him with one of the other captive women. After all, Nordwin only cares about claiming the woman who is in highest standing in the village or town or tribe that we Raiders plunder. She could be a Queen or simply the King's wife. She could be a High Priestess or just the Chief's virgin daughter. It is symbolic more than anything. A way to make freelance Raiders like myself bow to him. Nordwin takes the woman and his pick of the plunder. The rest is for the Raiders to share as spoils. It is a loose system that works well enough.

But what if it doesn't work so well for me this time, I wonder as I seat myself across the broad wooden table from Wendra and place my hands softly on the flat top. Still Wendra keeps her slow breathing steady, her smooth face stoic. I am alone with my thoughts, and as the longship cuts through the choppy North Sea, those thoughts drift to my other ships and the plunder they contain.

Plunder in the form of people, I remind myself as a dis-ease grips my throat. Wendra was right to notice the oddness of me taking the children and the elderly captive. Viking Raiders usually take only the women—and even then just the ones they fancy. In our lands of the North we do not have use for thousands of slaves. We fish and hunt for food and will always do that for ourselves. Our raiding parties are small and tight-knit, and we do not bloat our ranks with men taken as captives. What will Nordwin say when my longships enter port laden with not pots of gold but a village-full of English fisherfolk?! I could not even answer my men's questions about why I held them back from slaughtering the warriors and doing what they would with the womenfolk. I said it was by Nordwin's decree, but when we pull into shore they will know I lied.

By Thor, they may know I lied even *before* we stand in Nordwin's court, I think as I glance toward the door to make sure it is closed. Did Carab and the men see that this woman makes me weak? Do they know how my body yields to hers, how my heart beats with hers, how my soul pulls to hers? Do they know that I would kill for her, die for her, most certainly *lie* for her?

"You lied to me," she says softly, her lips barely moving, her eyes still closed.

"I lie to no one," I say, blinking away the thought that perhaps she can read my mind. Perhaps she is a High Priestess and not a Queen.

Now her eyelids flutter and she looks at me. "Another lie," she says with a small smile. She was pretty in the sun but is stunning in the shadows. I shift on the wooden bench, unsure how long I can control myself from burning every bridge and making her mine here and now. I cannot do it, of course. I cannot turn my men into traitors for my own needs. Many of my raiders have families (indeed, many have more than one family . . .), and Nordwin would slaughter their wives and children and feed their bodies to the fish.

I stay quiet. She is smart, and she knows that out here at sea I am King. She knows that when we weigh anchor I lose my power and so does she. Perhaps she has heard of Nordwin, perhaps not.

"I said but a few words to you," I say finally. "None were lies."

"You did not lie with words," she says. Her brown

eyes darken, her red lips tighten, her eyelashes catch the candlelight. "Just like you said a queen reveals herself through character and not a crown, so does a lie reveal itself through feelings and not words."

I frown and jut my jaw out. I am no fool, but this woman's words make my head hurt. What has she seen in my actions? What have I revealed to her wise brown eyes? I settle myself down and place my palms once more flat on the table. She glances at my fingers and then back into my eyes. The candle in the dull steel plate flickers from an unfelt breeze.

"So you *feel* I have lied?" I say with a raised eyebrow.

"I feel something," she says softly. She leans forward and blows out the candle, sending a tendril of black smoke towards me. The candles from the other tables cast her face in dark gold shadow, and a chill goes up my spine as I wonder where she leads me.

I search her eyes for an answer, but she gives me none. I have met every sort of woman in my travels, and many a seductress has tried her hand at bending my will. If she has heard stories of Nordwin she would know that if I touch her I will be executed for tainting the King's tribute, for elevating myself to Nordwin's status. It would be a symbolic act against the King, and I would be killed along with every last one of my men. Perhaps their families too. Is that where she leads me? Is it a cold, calculated game? Or does she speak truthfully when she says *I feel something*? Does she feel what I feel?

"Perhaps it is sea-sickness you feel," I say with a grin, slapping the table with both hands and making the mug of warm ale jump. Wendra does not jump, though.

"It is some kind of sickness," she says, keeping her gaze steady as she curls a strand of hair around her ear. My cock moves and my heart pounds and the heat of danger tightens my back. She plays me for a walking erection, a beast with balls where other men have brains. I should turn and walk out of here, lock her below decks until we pull into port, toss her at Nordwin's jeweled boots and set sail on the next raid just like I have always done.

"Salted fishmeat cures many a sickness," I say, glancing at the dried herring laid out on parchment at one end of the table. "And so does brown ale. If that does not work, try resting. The sun will set soon and we will reach the North shores by dawn."

I swallow as my throat tightens. "And if the sickness still bothers you, King Nordwin has men who might cure what I cannot."

"I have not heard of King Nordwin," she says, a hint of color darkening her cheeks. "Is he a good king?"

My eyes dart toward the closed door and then back into her eyes. Does she lie? Does she lay a trap for me? Does she hope I will speak against my King in front of my men?

"All Kings are good," I say flatly. "But if you hope to be his Queen, I fear that may not be in the stars for you."

Now the color drains from her face, and I know not what to make of her. I decide to make nothing of her, and without more words I stand and stride to the door. I stop before opening it and stare at the knotted wood. I burn to ask her what lie I revealed, but when I turn my head and see her eyes I know the answer and it is so clear I cannot be in her presence lest I break.

You will not be touched by me, I'd promised her.

That was the lie.

It was a lie because I already touched her.

Not in the flesh but in the spirit.

Because she knows the truth I will not admit:

That I spared her tribe because of her. She knows it and it means something to her. It touched her, and that means something to me.

And so I cannot see her again. Her fate is up to King Nordwin now. She can play her game with the "good" King. I have shown my weakness and now I will not step into the arena with her. I will not put my men's lives and families on the line to satisfy my pride or my loins or my heart or my soul. After all, I cannot be vanquished if I do not step into battle.

And so I tear my eyes away from her and grip the door handle so hard I almost rip the iron nails from the wood. I storm past my drunken men with fire in my eyes and darkness in my heart, and when I get to my chambers I am silently grateful that the other women are not on this ship. Who knows what I would do with this need that burns in me like the thunderbolts of Odin himself.

3
THE NEXT DAY
KING NORDWIN'S COURT
WENDRA

"A tribute fit for Odin himself," Wolruff declares after a stiff bow and a long, labored breath. I glance at the back of his head and then past him towards King Nordwin.

The King is short and wiry, with wisps of blond hair and pale blue eyes. A long nose that twists left, thin lips fixed somewhere between a sneer and a smile. He does not look like a good King. I did not expect him to be a good King.

Wolruff turns on his boot heel and walks past

me without looking into my eyes. But as he passes I see his chest tighten and his throat move, and
I feel that thing behind my breast, feel that intuition that made me think I could sway this Viking,
negotiate with him, vanquish him with words and
feelings and the swell of my breasts and the wetness of my lips and the warmth between my legs.

The memory of yesterday disgusts me, and I
tighten my buttocks and press my thighs together
as Wolruff's scent cuts through the perfumed air of
Nordwin's court. I acted like a common whore yesterday though I believed my own words, believed
that I felt something for my captor, that perhaps
I could turn him into my savior, that maybe I indeed had a sickness for which Wolruff was the cure.

My lips tighten into a smile as I remember the
last man I thought was a savior. I was a fool, and
he suffered for my error. And now here I am, pre-
sented as tribute to a thin-lipped, crooked-nosed
King who does not appear convinced that I am a
gift worthy of Odin.

"Do you believe I plan to *eat* her, Wolruff?" says
Nordwin, slumping in his gold-backed throne and
crossing one leg over the other knee. He wears
knee-high stockings of purple silk and light brown
leather sandals laced up past his spindly calves.

A murmur rises from the nobles at the front and the warriors at the back. I hear Wolruff stop a few paces beyond me.

"I do not understand," he says. "Of course I do not expect you to eat her."

"Then why did you fatten her up thus?" retorts the King, his dangling foot moving wildly as that sneer tightens into a smirk and the murmur rises to a roar.

My cheeks flush with anger and I hear Wolruff take three steps toward me and the King. I keep my eyes averted so the King will not see my rage. Already I sense the man seeks attention and approval, which means that any challenge or insult will be punished swift and harsh.

Wolruff stays silent but I hear his chain-mail armor stretch as he flexes his chest and broadens his shoulders. Again I get the sense that my intuition yesterday was not wrong, that perhaps if I had persisted I might have turned him to my side. Of course, it is too late now. Perhaps it was already too late yesterday. Perhaps my fate was written the day I overruled my intuition and married a man who now sleeps with the mermaids at the bottom of the sea.

"Maybe next time you will bring me a mermaid like I asked, Wolruff," says the King, looking around at his nobles. They touch their belts and laugh from their bellies. "Or wait—perhaps this creature has a tail beneath her skirts! Let us see. Come, Wolruff. Reveal the mermaid to us!"

I stiffen and turn my head halfway, my breath catching as I feel Wolruff tense up. He lets out a low growl that comes through as vibration and not sound. I hear his jawbone click and his knuckles crack. A spark of hope flickers in me, but it is quickly snuffed out by reason and common sense. If Wolruff could not be moved yesterday when there might have been a chance, he will not be moved today when there is no chance. This Viking has brains to go with that bulk, and he is too smart to sacrifice himself and perhaps his men for the pull of the heart. And anyway, what do I know about how the heart pulls?

"She is not a mermaid," Wolruff says coldly. "If the King is displeased with his tribute, there are many others we have taken captive. Perhaps I can—"

"Yes, I heard you captured many others," Nordwin snaps. "Old men wrinkled like prunes and gnarled like trees. Children who scream for breastmilk and the warmth of the bosom. Warriors who should be rotting on the battlefield instead of resting on my longships."

Wolruff clears his throat. "*My* longships," he says.

The King blinks and sticks his neck forward like a vulture. "What?"

"The longships," says Wolruff, this time a bit louder. "They are mine, King Nordwin. I pay tribute to my King like all Raiders, but the ships are mine and the men are mine."

Gasps rise like a chorus, and I frown at the red-and-gold carpet as I reconsider my belief about Wolruff's intelligence. I steal a sideways glance at him, still frowning. And immediately I look away to hide a smile.

Because I know what just went through his mind.

I know that he said more than what the court heard.

The ships are mine and the men are mine, he'd declared to his King. But his eyes whispered what his lips did not:

And so is she, said his eyes. *She too is mine.*

4
WOLRUFF

She too is mine, says my heart as it threatens to explode in my chest. I clench my fists and grind my teeth, wishing I could go back to yesterday and play my hand differently. I overruled my instinct and walked out of the food hall like a coward flees the battlefield. But the coward soon finds that his fortress walls offer no safety. How can they, when the battle is fought in your heart, lost and won in your soul?

And I am in danger of losing not just the battle but my life right now, it occurs to me as silence still as death falls over the court. Nordwin has executed men for less, and even though I spoke a truth that all Vikings know and accept, it sounded like a challenge, like I was questioning the King, perhaps even insulting him.

My gaze stays front and steady, but I am already scanning the court in case things call for action. My Vikings line the back of the royal hall, and I hear their boots on the smooth stone floor as they shift on their feet. Out on the seas they would stand behind me to the last man, to their last breath. Out here many of them would still stand with me without regard for consequence, and I wince inside at the pain from my poor judgment. The judgment of a fool. The judgment of a man who missed his chance yesterday and now tries to reach for a prize which is beyond his grasp.

"I *am* a mermaid," comes her voice through the clouds in my mind. I frown and cock my head when I see Wendra smiling wide and bright at the King, her back straight, curvy rump sticking up and out, breasts high like mountain peaks. "But I have no tail. Mermaids lose their tails when they are captured, you see. Set me free and my tail will grow back. And if you *do* set me free, I am bound by the Code of the Mermaids to grant you three wishes, Great King." She broadens the smile and bends her knee in playful respect, and when I see King Nordwin raise an eyebrow and then slowly lean back and touch his lip and smile, I hold my tongue and stand still as a rock as Wendra wields her ax, swings her sword, spins her web.

"Three wishes . . ." Nordwin says, tapping his lip and swinging his stocking'd foot. He glances at me and then back at her. I exhale when I realize Wendra just made him forget about my insult. She may have just saved my life. Does that not bind me to her? Does it not put me in debt to her? Am I not pledged by honor to serve her with my life until the debt is repaid?

I push the thought away. It is a dangerous thought, and I cannot trust myself to give it life. Perhaps I yearn for an excuse to do something that goes against all reason. Perhaps I ache to follow that feeling and take her as mine, do what my intuition urged when I first saw her walk out of the flames like a goddess reborn.

"All right, Magical Mermaid," says the King with a grin. "My first wish is to never die. To live forever. Like a god."

"It will be so," says Wendra with a wave of her hand and a flutter of her lashes. The nobles and warriors alike laugh and clap, and King Nordwin grins and looks around in glee.

"My second wish . . ." he says, narrowing his eyes at her, "is to sit upon the Throne of England."

Wendra blinks and swallows before composing herself and smiling. "One day you will sit upon the Throne of England," she says with a hand-wave that is less convincing. The gleam in Nordwin's blue eyes shines dull in a way I do not like. "And your third wish, Great King?"

King Nordwin stands and stretches. He looks around at his nobles and then up at the high ceiling of the Great Hall. "My third wish is to be taller," he says with a wink and a shrug to his audience. But that gleam in his eye worries me, and I open up my fist and flex my fingers in case I need to reach for my dagger. Nordwin holds his hand high above his head. "About this tall," he says. Then he looks down his crooked nose at Wendra and raises an eyebrow. "I am waiting, Mermaid. I do not feel myself growing. You are not by chance lying, are you? Playing me for a fool? A child in King's clothing? An idiot in a crown?"

Wendra somehow holds her smile and posture. "No, Great King. But remember what I said: I can only grant the wishes once I am set free."

Nordwin bites his lip and crosses his arms over his shimmering green tunic. "Ah, yes. The catch in

the story. The twist in the tale." He smiles thinly
and glances at the masked men of the Royal Guard
who stand by the throne. Very well. You shall be
set free, Mermaid. I cannot wait to feel myself grow
taller, sit upon the Throne of England, and live hap-
pily ever after for eternity." He whips his head toward the Royal Guard. "Set the Mermaid free," he
says casually. "Free her head from her tail and we
shall see if my wishes come true."

"No!" I roar, stepping forth even though I know
I cannot stand against the Royal Guard with just
a dagger. Perhaps with my battle-ax I could have
fought my way out, but the King does not per-
mit Vikings to carry heavy weapons in his court.
The Royal Guard advance, and the first one swings
his ax free and twirls it to loosen his arm. "No!" I
shout again, pulling out my dagger and holding
it up. Then I look at the King and call out with all
the authority I can summon. "Allow *me* to set her
free, King Nordwin. I will set her free. She is mine
to set free."

The Royal Guard stop and turn to the King. He
rubs his smooth chin and frowns down at me. Then
he nods and sighs and waves away his guards and
settles back into his throne to watch the show.

I exhale slow as my vision narrows to a tunnel

that gets smaller with every moment. I do not see a way out, and I turn to Wendra with a smile so heavy it hurts. My palm is wet against the leather-wrapped handle of my dagger that has slit more throats than there are heads in this hall. But cutting her soft skin is not even a thought in my mind. I step toward her, moving slow as the King and his court watch. I glance past her towards my men and blink slowly at my First Mate. It is an order to hold back, to stand down. This does not concern them. It is not their fight. It is not their fate.

"Perhaps I should have listened to you yesterday, Queen Wendra," I whisper as I let my gaze take in her beauty, let my nostrils inhale her sweetness, let my heart open so I can feel what I dared not admit. What does it matter now? In moments both she and I will be dead. I could save myself but it feels empty. I have already lost. I lost the battle yesterday when I walked away from the table, walked away from her, walked away from my fate.

"Listen to me now," she whispers, raising her head and exposing her beautiful bare neck. "Cut me clean across the front of the neck, deep through the fleshy middle but shallow near the sides where the blood pumps hard and hot. I will bleed for the audience but my heart will yet beat." She swallows and takes a breath, letting it out slow in a way that makes me shudder. "It will not beat for long, though." She speaks no more, but her eyes say so much. My heart finishes her sentence, and my eyes speak my answer.

We stare at each other and for a moment the walls melt away and the hall opens up to the sky and it is just the two of us, a Mermaid and a Viking, a man and a woman. But I blink and the moment is lost. The memory remains, though, and I know it is a memory of the future, of what can be real if my hand cuts clean, my blade cuts right, her heart beats strong enough . . . and for long enough.

Her brown eyes cut through me as I grip my dagger. It feels heavier than my battle-ax as I raise it to her throat. It catches the light from the chandelier, blinding me for a moment. I close my eyes and trust my hand, cutting through the air between us and praying to Thor and Odin and Freya and even Loki to guide my blade and grant me one wish.

One wish is all I ask, I say to the gods as the tip of my dagger touches her skin and opens up a thin line that feels like it is being cut in my own flesh, etched in my own heart.

My gut churns as Wendra gasps and sways and falls. I catch her easily around the waist, and in one quick move lift her into my arms. Her head hangs limp to one side, the blood red as a sunset. It trickles down her neck and onto my fingers, and I spin around towards the King to give him his show.

"Now I will return the Mermaid to the sea!" I proclaim with what I hope is dispassionate panache. Then, without waiting for the King to yea or nay my proclamation, I head for the gilded double-doors of the Great Hall, moving as fast as I dare, praying to those gods and goddesses to grant me this one wish, this one boon, this one gift.

This one woman.

5
__WENDRA__

Am I woman or ghost, I wonder as I look up at white mist. After blinking twice I see blue sky and smell sea salt. I take a breath and cough. Then I tense up as I swallow, waiting for the metallic taste of blood in my throat. There is none, and I almost sob in relief.

"A hair's width deeper and you would have drowned in your own blood," comes his voice from beside me. I turn my head and groan when I feel the sharp pain of my cut. He touches my cheek and shakes his head. "Do not move. Perhaps it will not leave a scar if you keep still until it heals."

"I am long past the point where I worry about

scars," I say, groaning again as my head pounds like Thor himself is hammering at it. "Water," I say hoarsely.

Wolruff stands and finally I see him. He's holding a wooden cup. I try to sit up but I cannot. He slides his hand beneath my back and raises me so I can drink. The water is warm but sweet. I smile at him and wince as he lowers me down to the rolled-up wool blanket that is my pillow.

"Where are we?" I say when I feel movement and realize we are on a ship.

Wolruff squints up at the sun and then looks down at me. "Heading Southwest, best I can tell. I did not track the stars last night." He goes quiet and I smile. He was tracking me last night, I know. Holding my head steady so the skin closed up faster. Watching my chest move to make sure I was breathing. Trickling water past my dry lips every hour. I remember none of that but know it like I know my own hand, like I know my own heart, like I know my own fate.

"What of my people?" I whisper after we share a comfortable silence broken only by the waves lapping against the wooden hull of the longship.

"They were still captive on my anchored ships," Wolruff says. "I ordered my men to untie them and let them set sail. I know not where they go." He pauses. "I know not if King Nordwin will send ships after them. But they know how to sail and there are warriors amongst them. They can take care of themselves. They are not my concern. Nor are they yours. Not anymore. You are a Queen without a country now, Wendra. You are dead to the world. If King Nordwin gets word that you are alive, not only will he send ships after us, but he could well imprison or even execute my men, perhaps even their families. We are lost souls now, Wendra. Drifters. Wanderers. Ghosts."

I blink as I take in the enormity of what he has done for me. A tiny voice whispers that I should not forget that all of this was *started* by him, that had this Viking not sailed his longships up the river delta and into my village, neither of us would be here. Then another voice—this one not so tiny—whispers that perhaps it is not such a bad thing that I am here and he is here and we are alive and floating with the tides, sailing with the wind.

"Why?" I say, not sure what I ask, not sure of whom I ask it.

"You know why," he says, answering my question and perhaps his own question in the only way that makes sense.

I nod. I do know why but cannot say it. I cannot say what I felt when I saw his shadow, smelled his scent, sensed his soul. "In my tribe marriages were arranged at birth," I say as I watch the clouds make shapes above me. I know not why I tell him this but I cannot stop the words. "They would place newborn babes in the calm shallows of a pool and watch how they drifted. There was no tide and no current, but still you would see patterns emerging, witness children drawn to one another as if by unseen forces. It was the pull of nature, they say. Matches ordained by fate."

Wolruff grunts. "Then clearly we are not fated to be married, because I do not float. My bones are heavy like iron. If that were the custom of my people, I would have dropped like a rock, sunk as a stone." He chuckles. "Though perhaps it means my match is a mermaid," he says. He raises an eyebrow at me and twists his mouth into a half-smile. "Which reminds me: Do I get three wishes now that I have set you free?"

I smile even though it hurts. "Don't you want to see if your King Nordwin has grown taller before trusting in my powers?"

"He will sit upon the Throne of England before he grows taller."

"And he will need to live forever if he hopes to claim England's throne," I add.

We laugh together and then I wince. Wolruff places his palm upon my brow and frowns. "There is a fever."

"A fever is good. It is the body fighting its way to balance." He holds the cup to my lips and I drink. Then I reach up and touch his forehead. It is warm but not with fever. I think of that old matchmaking ritual of my people. Did we drift toward each other on the tides of time, the sea of space? I had no match when the ritual was performed on me, the elders said. It meant I was special, they said. Born to be alone, came the whispers when I grew old enough to understand them. Of course, soon I grew bold enough to ignore them, taking a husband even though I never gave myself to him. He drowned on our wedding night, drunk on the fermented nectar from the carrow-root. He drowned in that very pool where the babies are floated to their fates. My fate was to be alone, and I decided then I was foolish to fight it.

So what chance do I have that this Viking has changed my fate, I wonder as I draw my hand back from his rough skin and resist the urge to look into his eyes. I see how he looks at me. I feel how he wants me. Nothing stops him from taking me. Perhaps he will do just that.

"What would you have me do when you are healed?" he says softly. "Your village is burned. Your people may return there, but I do not think they will. I think they will settle in a safer village on England's coast. Build new homes closer to the protection of London."

I blink and look away. Thoughts of home make my heart heavy, but where else can I go? What else can I do? Sail the seas on a Viking longship for eternity? Live off fish and rainwater?

"If I return to England, King Nordwin might hear I still live," I say.

"He may hear of it anyway. My men know it. They are loyal, but there may be questions about where my ships have gone."

"They *are* your ships, are they not?"

"Yes. So perhaps it will be forgotten before anyone bothers to ask. King Nordwin is easily distracted. Something new will occupy his attention. Rumors will pass like a storm, leaving the seas smooth like glass after a time."

I close my eyes and then open them when a heavy raindrop hits my nose. I blink as the rain comes like beads, wetting my face and hair. Wolruff lifts me off the deck like a doll, swiftly carrying me below. It is dark and stuffy under decks, the air stale and damp. The stench of dried fish and flat ale nauseates me, and I feel my fever rise.

"You will be safe here," Wolruff says, kicking open the heavy wooden door to what must be his chambers. It smells like him, and I relax when he lays me upon the hard straw bed. He strokes my hair like I am a child, and then he twists his face when the wind blows the rain against the thick wooden hull. The rain hits like spears, and when the thunder shakes the ship and the wind whistles through the small spaces between the logs and planks of the longship, Wolruff turns and storms toward the door. "I must take down the sails," he says over his shoulder. "In this wind they could snap the masts like twigs."

As he says it we heard a crack like a tree falling in the forest, and Wolruff is gone like lightning. I hear his heavy boots go up the steps, and I close my eyes and try not to think about my fate, about what happened when I tried to make my own fate by taking a husband. Is this the goddess herself reminding me that *she* writes my fate and not I? Am I being punished for daring to reach for a destiny that is not mine to have?

The wind wails as my fever rises, and soon I cannot see the dark walls of the Viking's chambers. My eyelids flutter and my lips move without sound. Saliva pools at the sides of my mouth, and I feel a trickle down my neck.

Soon the trickle thickens, and I frown and try to see if I am bleeding again. I touch my neck and look at my fingers. My hand drips wet, but it is not blood. Then I feel more wetness, this time on my forehead and nose. I look up and gasp when I see water pouring through the ceiling.

I sit up and swing my legs off the bed. My stomach lurches and my head spins, but I know I must go above decks. Another mast cracks above, and suddenly I fear for Wolruff. My mind takes me back to when I found my husband face down in that shallow pool on our wedding night, and now I am running up the stairs that are soaked dark with seawater.

When I emerge I am almost taken by the wind, but I hold on to the wooden post at the top of the stairs and search for Wolruff. I see him bare-chested and bronzed, his muscles straining as he furiously brings down a heavy sail from the aft mast and moves on to the next. I do not call to him. If we lose all the masts in the storm, we are good as dead. We will drift with the tides until we one day meet our end on the jagged rocks that hide just beneath the surface all along the English coastline.

The wind whips rain at my face, but I hold tight and narrow my eyes. It is still mid-day but the clouds make it dark as a moonless night. The once-blue sea is gray like sin, and with every swallow I taste the salt in my throat. It is almost like the rain is saltwater, I think as I glance up and then out across the bow. The waves are so high they come over the sides like it is a rowboat, but that does not concern me as much as what I see past the bow.

"Wolruff!" I scream when I realize what I am looking at. I wipe the water from my face and look again. "Wolruff! We are upon the shore! We are being pushed aground! We are—"

We strike the rocks and I am thrown backwards down the stairs. I tumble and roll, somehow landing below decks without breaking my neck. My left leg is twisted beneath me, and when I try to stand I scream and fall back down. Then I see movement at the top of the stairs, and my heart calms when I see Wolruff. His hands are cut from the rough ropes lashing the sails, and blood mixed with rainwater drips from his fingertips.

I try to stand once more, but fall again. This time it is not from the pain of my leg. I fall because the hull has been breached and the sea comes through like a river, striking me with force and fury. Wolruff roars and starts down the stairs, but before he takes the first step a shadow falls over him and I scream a warning he cannot hear.

The mast crashes down upon his back like a silent stalker, its ambush bringing Wolruff down with breathtaking swiftness. I blink and stare as the water rises past my hips, unable to believe that he is gone. Did I just kill another man that I dared to believe might be mine? Is my love a curse? My touch poison? My whisper more deadly than an arrow?

The saltwater burns the fresh cut on my neck, and for a moment I want to sink myself beneath the surface, end this wretched lonely life just like I started it: Alone. My knees buckle and my legs shake, but somehow I keep my head above water and breathe like there is still something for which to breathe, still a destiny for which to endure, still a fate for which to fight.

And so even as my heart pulls me down like a weightstone, something else in me reaches out and grasps a heavy splinter the size of a small tree. I cling to it as the water rises, carrying me upwards with it as the ship sinks lower. Moments later I am being washed over the flooded decks, off the sloping side of the listing ship, into the dark waters that churn with angry froth.

I whirl through the waves, spin through the swell, my fingernails broken and bleeding as I claw at my splintered raft and hang on like I am cursed to never die. I see the longship bent and broken on the wicked black rocks as I rise on the swell of the ocean. The last mast comes down slow and silent like an old tree, and then the longship is gone and Wolruff is gone and I am alone again.

Alone like always.

Alone like forever.

6
ONE YEAR LATER
WOLRUFF

It has taken forever, but I am finally able to swing my battle-ax once more. My back is twisted like an old tree, but my strength has returned and although I do not stand as straight as before, at least I still stand.

"What of you, Wendra?" I whisper to the sea as I stand bare-chested on the rocky beach and swing my battle-ax like I fight unseen demons. "Do you still stand? Do you still breathe? Do you still . . ."

The words catch in my throat, and I swing my ax so hard I feel the pull in my shoulder and the pain in my back. I grit my teeth and stretch my chest, looking up at the cold blue steel of the North sky and searching for a sign from the gods. Something to relieve the tightness in my throat that comes not from my broken body but my lonely heart.

"You failed her, Wolruff," I growl, finally letting the heavy axhead drop into the packed sand. "You failed yourself. Failed your own fate. If only you'd seized the moment when she offered herself to you aboard your own longship. But no. You held true to vows of allegiance to a man you do not respect, a weak King who would have killed her and killed you and then feasted on pheasant before your blood turned cold."

I drag my ax along the beach as I wander aimlessly, like I have done day after day, month after month. The gods have no respect for a man who does not rise when he is called, and so how can I respect myself any longer?

The wind picks up and I stop and gaze out over the gray sea. A hundred times I have considered walking into the surf until I am no more. Perhaps I will wake up and see my mermaid smiling at me from her watery grave. Perhaps she will whisper that my one wish has come true.

"It is true," comes a familiar voice from behind

me. I do not turn, though. I have spent so much time alone that voices come and go like the breeze. "You have indeed gone mad."

Finally I turn, and a smile comes to my dry lips when I see Carab, my First Mate from a time when I was a Viking Captain and I commanded longships and I raided and plundered and conquered. Oh, what joy I felt in those days. And then I met her, and now look at me.

I swallow the anger that rises in me now and then like a serpent that lives in the darkest part of my soul. As much as I yearn to see Wendra again, sometimes the thought sickens me to the toes. There are countless myths of the hero being derailed from his destiny by a trickster in female form, a temptress sent by the gods, a test of will and strength that I have failed. But it is not her fault. It is mine. If there is anger and hate, then let it be aimed at myself.

"My Captain and Commander," says Carab, stopping in the sand before me and bowing his head in respect. He glances at my axhead covered in wet sand. Then he looks at my twisted posture and broken back. He blinks and moves his jaw and looks away.

I smile ruefully. "Do not call me thus. I cannot be a Captain without ships. I cannot be a Commander without standing straight."

"We have new ships," says Carab. He looks at my ax again, his gaze travelling up my thick arms that still bulge with muscle. "And so long as you can still swing that heavy ax straight enough, we will follow you into battle again. What say you, Wolruff?"

My grip tightens around the warm wooden ax-handle. I raise the heavy club over my head, frowning as it strikes me as odd that on the first day I am able to swing my ax, Carab shows up like a messenger from the gods. I glance up at the clear sky, then back over to the horizon. Am I being offered another chance? A way back from the wilderness? Back to what, though?

Back to your fate, comes the answer on the breeze. Will you seize the chance this time? Or will you shift on your feet and ask a hundred silly questions, rub your jaw and worry about the danger, scratch your elbow and grumble about the risks, pick your arse and ask about the rewards?

"We need a Captain, Wolruff," says Carab. "We will not sail under another man's command. What say you?"

I start to think and then stop. "I say yes," I say as I try to push away the hope of something that cannot pass, try to forget the one wish I had made a year ago. "If I can stand, I can sail. If I can swing my ax, I can plunder. Where do we raid this time?

France, perhaps? It has been some time since we pillaged the French coast. Perhaps they have forgotten about us." I twirl my ax like it is a toothpick. "Perhaps we should remind them why Vikings are feared all across Europe."

Carab grins and nods. "The French fools will not have forgotten, Wolruff. They will still remember us when we storm into their ports and steal their gold and fuck their women until their bloodlines change forever. That will have to wait, though. Our new ships are gifts from King Nordwin, and we sail as part of his fleet. To England. Right up the River Thames to the great City of London. We are to sack the Tower and take the Palace."

I frown and cock my head. I have been on my own too long. No news reaches me out here on the remote Northern coast. But this news cannot be real. Yes, our longships are built to sail up rivers and back out to sea, but to sail into the lion's den is madness. Certainly King Nordwin is capable of madness, but not this sort of madness. He may have grand dreams, but he does not have the courage to chase them. Certainly not up the River Thames and against an army vastly more powerful.

I lean close and sniff the air around Carab. It does not smell good, but nor does it smell like ale.

"I am not drunk," says Carab, grinning and swiping at the air between us. "Have you not heard the news?"

"What news?"

"King Nordwin," says Carab, blinking and shaking his head like either he does not believe I have not heard the news or he does not believe the news at all. "Last month he . . . he grew."

I furrow my brow and blink away a pain behind my left eye. "What do you mean *he grew*?"

Carab holds his hand above his head and looks up. "I mean he grew taller. Tall just like he wished one year ago. His wish came true, Wolruff. So now he believes that *all* three wishes are destined to come true. He believes he will sit upon the Throne of England. He believes he will live forever. Perhaps that woman really *was* a mermaid, eh, Wolruff?"

"Mermaid . . ." I mutter, mindlessly repeating Carab's words as my vision blurs and my heart beats wild. The memory of that day one year ago is burned deep like a brand in my mind, and I stagger back as Carab's words lights it up again. The King grew taller? Could it be true? And if so, what does it mean? Did Wendra speak the truth about the wishes? If she did, I do not believe she *knew* she spoke the truth.

It cannot be true, I tell myself as I turn from Carab and stroke my beard. I think back to every word

Wendra said to the King a year ago, and then a chill goes up my twisted spine.

The wishes will only come true when I am set free, she'd said.

The words had been spoken in jest, I'd thought. But what if they weren't? What if Wendra really *has* been set free?

And now my heart sinks in a whirlpool of despair and the truth pulls me down.

Because where is a mermaid most free?

If not at the bottom of the sea . . .

7
CITY OF LONDON
WENDRA

"London is wetter than the bottom of the sea!" I say with a smile as the rain pours off the brim of my hat. Some gets down my collar, but I care not. Soon I'll be dry in my home, warm near my fire, safe with my secrets.

Not that anyone in this bustling, smoky city cares about another's secrets. And not that my secrets are particularly interesting to anyone else. My life is not particularly interesting either, but I am alive and that is something. It is the only thing.

I get to the narrow three-story building where I have a room at the top of the stairs. There are mice in the walls and spiders on the ceiling, but they are my friends now and I love them like children. I speak to them earnestly, and sometimes I believe they answer me.

I lift my dripping skirts off my muddy shoes as I climb up the wooden stairs. I am warmed by the time I enter my room, but I start the fire anyway. I like to look at the flames. Fire is the opposite of water, and I can no longer look at water without being taken back to that dark day when the goddess reminded me that my fate was not mine to command, that my destiny is to die alone and so any man who lingers in my path will be taken by the water, drowned in the deep, swallowed by the sea.

"I see you," I whisper to the white mouse who sticks his nose from his hole. His whiskers twitch and he pulls back out of sight. I sigh and sit back on my little wooden stool and rub my hands together to dry them. I sigh again when I feel how rough my palms have become. I spend my days cleaning floors and scrubbing walls for the other tenants in the building. In return the landlord lets me stay in this room. It has been a year since I was rescued by fisherfolk and brought back to England. A year since I came to London and found work and a place to stay. It should have felt like the start of a new life, but somehow it feels temporary, like it is just something to do until . . . until I do not know what. I cannot even admit what I await. Admitting it would prove my madness. Better to smile at the walls and talk to the mice. What say, Mouse? What am I waiting for? The Vikings to storm the city, sail up the river, the ghost of Wolruff standing at the helm of his longship, my name on his lips?

I am about to cackle out a laugh but stop. "What is that?" I say, frowning at I hear shouts come through my narrow window. I rise and walk over as the shouts rise to a steady roar that reminds me of the ocean. I touch the thin scar on my neck and then squint through the glass. It is too fogged-up to see past, and I sigh and pull open the window.

I recoil at the smell of fresh smoke, and when I poke my head out I gasp at the sight of flames rising from buildings along the River Thames! The rain has stopped and the smoke billows black like tar, but even through the cloud I can make out something that feels like it is from a dream . . . perhaps from a fantasy, maybe from my madness.

"Vikings," I whisper, touching my scar and staring at the longships sailing in single file up the river. Long-haired men hurl flaming torches from the decks, send spears flying through the air like arrows as English soldiers scramble and scurry along the banks. "What . . . what in heaven's name do they think they're doing? Are they lost? Have they gone mad?"

I watch in disbelief and even amusement, and then my eyes go wide when one of the longships veers towards the riverbank and comes alongside with soft precision that reminds me how skilled these men are with ships that seem far too large for such narrow waterways. I watch as Viking Raiders leap off the ship like pirates. The smoke hurts my eyes but I cannot look away. Something draws my gaze to that longship that appears to have broken formation and come alongside.

I keep staring until my eyes burn, and through the smoke I make out a large man standing near the railing. He does not stand straight but leans to the left. From his right hand swings a battle-ax that looks bigger than the Tower of London. It is dark and smoky and I cannot see his face, but something about his shadow strikes a note of familiarity in me.

"I've seen that shadow before," I murmur as I touch my neck again and close my eyes as I'm taken back to when I saw Wolruff's shadow before I ever saw his face. I swallow hard and shake my head, forcing myself to push away the hope that I know will only be dashed when I see his face, see that it is not him.

"Because it *cannot* be him," I mutter as my scar burns like a fresh cut. I can almost feel Wolruff's rough hands on my throat when he cut me just right, his blade slicing true like it was guided by the goddess, wielded by fate. I swallow hard and shake my head again, and when I open my eyes the man is gone.

I lean out the window and look for him, but more buildings are burning and soldiers are riding onto the scene and there is shouting and screaming and swearing and my heart drops and my soul sighs and I pull away and slam the window shut and sit down on my stool and stare into the flames. My hands tremble and my lips quiver, and I think about that old matchmaking ritual and I wonder if Wolruff and I would have drifted towards each other if we'd been placed upon the still waters together.

Then I wonder if our lives are those waters and our choices are the waves, if perhaps I got it wrong a year ago, if maybe the goddess was sending a message different from the one I saw in the shipwreck, felt in the flames.

Maybe the message isn't to bow my head and accept my fate.

Maybe it's to stand tall and seize it instead.

Maybe the misfortune wasn't a warning but a test.

A test that maybe . . .

Just maybe . . .

I have not yet failed.

8
__WOLRUFF__

King Nordwin may fail to take the city in the end," I say through a wild smile as I leap off my ship and plant my heavy boots on solid ground. "But we will take some of the city with us. We are Vikings, and we will pillage and plunder and lay waste to London before sailing away with gold and girls just like we have always done. Onward, men!"

My men roar with glee as they set fire to buildings and shatter windows and break down doors. They rush into storefronts and come out with fistfuls of coin and armfuls of furs. Some are draped with silks and jewels, others saddled with leather goods and finery. Some fight English soldiers with delight, others merrily roar gibberish at the locals just for fun. My orders were to follow Nordwin's fleet to the heart of the City to sack the Tower and take the Palace, but I am not built to follow orders.

Still, I did not plan to pull my longship ashore right here, I think as I swat three English soldiers away with the blunt shaft of my battle-ax. I kick another in the chest and grab one by the hair, dragging him like a doll as I stomp through the streets and join in the fun. Our attack came with stealth and surprise, and even though I know King Nordwin has neither the numbers nor the skill to defeat the English army in London, the audacity of sailing our ships from the North Sea right up the gullet of the Thames certainly has them rocking on their heels.

"Hell, who knows," I mutter as I knock two Englishmen's heads together and watch their eyeballs turn upwards as they go down like sacks of dried cod. "Maybe the King's wishes really *will* come true. After all, he *did* look taller when I sighted him."

I lose sight of my men as I turn down a small street and find myself suddenly alone. Again it occurs to me how strange it was to find my longship pulling out of formation even though the river's current flows strong and straight. It reminds me of how it came to pass that one year ago I sailed my fleet of three longships into that small fishing village on the English coastline. The village was hidden upriver from the delta, and it was almost accidental that we found it. The wind changed suddenly and violently, filling my sails and turning my bow.

Turning it toward her.

I turn in the empty street, looking up and seeing stars even though the air is thick with smoke. The stars sparkle like they see me too, and I frown up at them and keep turning, my ax in my hand, my back straighter than it has been in a year. Every sailor learns that the stars drift like the seas, but if you know what to look for they will lead you home like the tides. Are the stars leading me somewhere? Or did I lose my way that night a year ago when I turned my back on destiny, shook my head at fate, walked away from Wendra?

Somewhere down the street a window creaks open and then slams shut. It breaks me from my trance, and now I hear the shouts of my men as more English soldiers march in to join in the game. In the distance I hear the roar of battle, and I know Nordwin's fleet has begun their siege on the Tower of London. With a sigh I glance up at the quiet buildings once again before readying myself to return to the world of men and mayhem.

Footsteps sound to my left, and I whip around and raise my ax. It is one of my Vikings, and I watch as he races down the street with a flaming torch and tosses it wildly at one of the buildings. Then he is gone like a ghost, and I shake my head and wonder if I just imagined it.

But I hear the crackle of fresh flame and smell the pungent black smoke. The building is stone and will not burn, but the front door of the building is dry wood and it goes up like tinder. I watch as the flames snake into the gaping hole and lick at the wooden staircase before climbing like it has a mind of its own. I glance up at the narrow building and rub my beard. It looks dark and deserted. The rest of the street looks deserted too, and I suspect people have fled towards the Tower, hoping for sanctuary behind the fortress walls and the English battlements.

I lower my ax and also my gaze, but then another window opens—this one in the narrow building with the burning staircase. I look up and raise an eyebrow. The window stays open but I do not see anyone. Then a woman's head sticks out and I blink and frown. Night has fallen and the flames cast dark shadows and she could be anyone or no-one or everyone. I glance at the burning staircase and back up at the woman. No other windows in the building are open. She is the only one who did not flee the building. Why did she stay?

"Perhaps she has a death wish or maybe she can fly," I grunt, forcing myself to look away. In a hundred raids I have taken thousands of warrior lives, but we Vikings do not slaughter the unarmed and defenseless. We take women as brides and mistresses and playthings and pets, but we do not kill the ones we leave behind. We love to burn like the demon-hordes we are reputed to be, but we make enough noise and commotion that people know to flee their homes when we sail our ships into their lives with burning torches in our hands and mischief in our eyes. Common sense tells me that over the years some of the innocent and defenseless have died in my raids, but I did not know it and did not see it and certainly did not command it. That makes a difference. It makes all the difference.

And that means I cannot walk away from this woman with no face and no name and probably no damned sense. If I leave her to burn or leap to her death it is like I wielded the ax myself, cut her throat with my own dagger.

Smoke pours from the openings along the gullet of the building. I hear the wood groan and sigh as the flames eat the stairs like a monster making a meal. Let us hope she can indeed fly, I think grimly. Because that is the only way down from her perch.

In the distance the battle for London rages, but here it is still like a graveyard, quiet as death. Here it is just me and a nameless, faceless woman trapped in a tower, and my bearded face broadens in a smile as I sniff the smoky air. I glance up at the stars once again, and once again they shine through the smoke and sparkle like they speak to me. Are the gods giving me another chance? Are they testing me once again? I failed to save Wendra a year ago, and although I would have been happy to die, some-how I was washed ashore with a broken back and a shattered heart. If the gods spared me even after I failed, then perhaps I have not yet failed! Perhaps they test me again with a woman I do not know and do not love. Perhaps they want to see what kind of man I am.

What kind of Viking.

What kind of hero.

And so I lick my lips and grip my ax, my eyes snapping into focus as I study the stone facade. Every Viking boy learns how to climb the tall masts of a longship as soon as he learns to walk, and even though I am no boy but heavy like a boulder, I still can get to the top of a mast as fast as the wiriest of my men.

Or at least I could, I think as I feel the pull in my twisted back where the broken bones fused and made me look like a monster. Again I study the stone outer walls, and although the stone is smooth and the workmanship tight, there is always a path to be found, just like any sea can be conquered, any river can be navigated, any odds can be overcome. If there is no path up those walls, then I will *make* a path up those walls.

And so I step to the walls and look up at the open window. Starlight blazes down on me like the gods are smiling. I think of that child's tale where a trapped princess lets down her hair for the prince like a ladder, and I chuckle at the horror of any princess who sees a hefty prince the size of a bull about to put his full weight on her plaits.

Wisps of smoke come from her window, and I drop the smile and raise my ax. I bring down the heavy axhead hard and straight, the Viking steel cutting through stone and lodging deep. I grunt and pull myself up, jamming my toes into the narrow ornamental border that gives me just enough leverage to dislodge my ax and strike another blow, build my bridge slow and steady, storm my tower with brute strength and Viking will, prove myself in an empty street, for a nameless woman, with no witnesses but the gods.

"Though perhaps my Wendra watches from her heavenly perch amongst the angels and goddesses," I whisper as I pass the first set of windows and use the ledge to rest a moment. My back twitches and throbs, and I feel the fused spine strain at the seams. But although I am twisted I am no longer broken, and I know I will get to the top of the tower.

Getting down, however, I think with a grunt and a grin as sweat beads on my brow . . . now *that* could be a problem.

9
__WENDRA__

"This could be a problem," I say calmly as I stand at my open door and watch the flames march up the stairs like an uninvited dinner guest. I close the door and bite my lip before hurrying to the window and pushing it open.

The night is cold and the air is smoky. In the distance I hear the cries of men and the clash of swords, but my street is silent and empty. The other tenants of the building fled when the Vikings landed, heeding the calls of the town-criers to head to the Tower of London. I heeded nothing but perhaps my heart.

My heart that clearly yearns to stop beating.

I lean out the window and look up and down the street. Earlier I noticed a man standing in the street, but he is gone now. The man was big and he carried an ax. I could not see his face, but he was large and leaned to one side like his back was twisted--just like the man on the longship. For a moment I'd almost allowed myself to believe in the unbelievable, but then I'd remembered that not even a child would believe a story where fate time and time again brings two people together to see what will happen.

To see if *anything* will happen.

"Is that why I stayed in the building when all others fled?" I wonder out loud as the smoke creeps in through the sides of the door. "Is this how I pass fate's test? By testing the limits of faith? By believing that perhaps, just perhaps there is a chance that—"

The sound of metal on stone distracts me, and when I look down I see something moving near the window ledge two levels down. The smoke from the stairs clouds the air black, and I cannot see clearly. I squint into the smoke, and then I gasp when the glint of steel winks back at me. It is an axhead, and I gasp again when I see that whoever wields it is climbing up the side of the building, forging his own ladder in the hard stone, creating his own path up the wall like how a Viking sails his long-ship blindly upriver without knowing if he will be able to turn around and sail back out.

I stare down as my heart beats like a rabbit, and when the man's thick arms come into view and the ax strikes true beneath my window, I close my eyes tight and shake my head hard and tell myself that it can't be him, that it won't be him, that he's dead and even if he were alive he could not be here. *How* could he be here?! *Why* would he be here?!

I keep my eyes closed, and I feel the man's shadow cast upwards against my window by the flames from below. Now his scent comes to me, and my lips tremble as I taste the salt of the ocean, smell the musk of whale-oil, inhale an aroma that has stayed with me for a year, perhaps longer, maybe even forever.

"Wendra," comes his voice through the distant shouts of battle and the nearby hiss of flame. I touch my lips and wonder if I speak aloud, think aloud, wish aloud. But it is not my voice, and when I look down I see the man's head from above

He faces the wall and I cannot see his eyes nor his nose or mouth. He does not see me, and I wonder if I imagined my name on the night wind that has started to blow out of the north. But then my name sounds again, and I frown and then blink when I realize the man calls my name to himself!

"Wendra, are you watching?" he mutters as he hangs from his ax-handle and digs his boot-toes into the thin ornamental ledge that circles the stone facade. "Do you see me, Wendra?" he says again like he speaks to the stone.

"I see you, Wolruff," I whisper down to him. I know it cannot be him, that when he looks up and I see his eyes it will not be him. But for this one moment the fantasy is so real I almost believe it, and my hand goes to my neck and I shiver when I feel that scar from a year ago.

Now the man stops and turns his head left and then right. Slowly he turns his head upwards, and I stare down into eyes green like the ocean, a face scarred like a canyon, a beard rough like a stormy sea. We gaze upon each other like neither of us can believe it is real. It is a trick of the smoke. An illusion of the night. A mirage of the mind.

"Wendra?" he says, his face twisting into a frown, his eyelids opening and closing quickly and many times.

"Wolruff?" I say, cocking my head and wondering

if we both died in that shipwreck and this is how heaven works, how the afterlife plays out what was unfinished in the world of the flesh.

Now the smoke rises from below Wolruff and from behind me, and suddenly I am taken back to that moment when the mast cracked and broke his back, when the angry seas swept him one way and blew me the other, when it seemed like fate conspired not to bring us together but to split us apart, not as a test but simply as torment. Could the gods be so cruel as to bring us together again for one last look before ripping us apart—this time forever?

As if in reply, there is a sound from where his axhead holds the stone, and I look and then gasp when I see the blade move like it is coming loose!

"Wolruff!" I shout, reaching my arm out even though should he take it I would be pulled to my death along with him. "The ax . . . it comes loose!"

Wolruff follows my gaze and his eyes widen when he sees his blade pulling loose. He glances at my outstretched arm and snorts like it is a joke. But I hold my arm steady and look into his eyes. The ax-blade is almost out, and if it gives way he dies. Of course, if he lets go of the ax and takes my arm we both die. I cannot hold his weight. It would be absurd. Beyond reason. Impossible.

"But us being here is absurd," I whisper down to him, my thoughts becoming words like how a river flows to the sea. "Us being here is beyond reason. Us being here is impossible. Still we are here, though. Still we are alive and in this moment, looking into one another's eyes, faced with a choice that only a fool would make. So take my hand, you foolish, wonderful Viking. Let us answer the call. Let us challenge the gods that test us. Let us meet the eye of the goddesses who watch us. Take my hand, Wolruff. Take my hand."

And as I say it, the ax-head pulls out from the wall and everything stops.

Everything stops like the gods and goddesses are holding their breath, watching with both delight and dread, waiting to see what their human puppets will do. After all, this is how the gods and goddesses amuse themselves, is it not? They poke and prod, push and pull, tease and torment.

"But in the end they are not in control," I whisper as I see the light in Wolruff's eyes, like he just saw the same secret I did, that the gods love the game because they do not control it. We control it even though it seems absurd, impossible, beyond reason.

And that's the point.

That's the test.

Because the only way it works is if we *both* make the choice.

I must choose to risk my life and hold my arm out . . .

And he must choose to take it.

We both have to give up ourselves before we can have each other.

Because that's what it takes to seize your forever, claim your fate, vanquish your Viking.

So as we smile in the stillness of the moment, as the world starts to spin again, as our past and future merge into one point of infinite power, Wolruff lets go of the falling ax, reaches his big paw out, and takes my hand.

10

WOLRUFF

I take her hand and launch myself up toward the open window, gliding as if on the wings of the divine dove who brought word of new land after the great flood. My body feels lighter than a single feather on that dove, and my heavy boots tap soft and nimble against the stone. It is impossible but it is real and I believe it. I know I am pulled up by not the strength of our bodies but the power in our hearts. The power of our choice.

The choice to listen.

The choice to trust.

The choice to believe.

Now I am at the window and I hurl myself through

the opening as reality comes smashing into us like a hail-wind. She screams as my body slams into hers, and I grab her and pull her close as we crash into the room.

My body cushions hers as we land on a low table, shattering the wood like an old tree. The splinters drive deep into my back, reminding me that we are returned to the realm of the flesh, the world of blood and bone. I pull her close and cradle her head. We pant and stare. No words can be spoken because what happened cannot be spoken of in words.

Outside the door the stairs burn. Outside the building the battle rages. But here it is just the two of us. We burn with a different sort of flame. We fight a different sort of battle. A battle that is not won yet.

Not until I claim my queen. Plunder my prize. Seize my siren.

I stroke her cheek with my thumb and look upon her beauty like I have never seen it before even though it was all I saw in my dreams the past year. She parts her lips as if to speak but says not a word. This is not a time for words. It is not a time for thought. I cannot hesitate. Twice before the gods denied me because I turned away. This time I do not turn. I do not flinch. I do not stand down.

"You are mine, Wendra," I whisper, cupping her cheek and running my thumb over the smooth bump of her scar. "I knew it when I first saw you. I knew it when we faced each other in the food hall. I knew it when we stood before the King. I knew it when my blade touched your sweet skin. I knew it when the stormwinds broke my back. I knew it when I took your hand and our love pulled me in."

Wendra blinks away tears and her lips tremble and her body shivers as it presses down on mine. "You seem to know a lot for an ax-wielding Viking," she says. "What else do you know?"

"This. I know this," I growl, leaning close and running my nose delicately along her cheek, sniffing her like a beast of prey. The blood rushes to my head and my heart and my loins all at once, and I shudder as a power greater than I have known burns through me. My lips touch her cheek lightly as my hand tightens around the back of her neck. She shudders and I move closer to her lips. She smells like the sea after a storm, fresh and vibrant, churning with energy, roiling with joy. My cock throbs and my heart pounds, and I swear I feel the gods and goddesses watching us in muted silence as they wait. My mouth twists in a smile when I decide that the gods are no longer in control. Our choice to believe the unbelievable and accept the impossible has made us divine. We have fought and we have won. Do what you will, gods.

As if in answer comes a great crash outside the door. I know the stairs have collapsed, leaving a fiery pit outside the front door, like the gods have opened up a portal to the Underworld. Now they laugh and congratulate each other and sit back on their ephemeral thrones with self-satisfied smiles. But Wendra and I smile back at them. We smile because now we know how fate plays the game. We smile because now we know how to play it too.

And so, trapped in our tower with no way out, I look up into her eyes and bring my lips to hers.

And I kiss her.

By the gods and goddesses, I kiss her.

11

<u>WENDRA</u>

He kisses me with the power of the tide, slow but with hidden strength that sends ripples through my body. I heard the stairs crash down outside, and I know we have no way out. Somehow it matters not, though. Somehow I am ready to believe in anything now. Ready to believe in that old ritual of my people, that fate is like the tide, destiny like the current, that two fated souls will be brought together again and again like the waves to the shore.

And so I put all thoughts of escape out of my mind and kiss him back. I give myself to the moment and to forever, and as the kiss lights me up like a starburst, I see in my mind's eye that one moment and forever are the same thing, that time and space are like the sea and the sky, that love is like the horizon-line between the two, that magical threshold where sea and sky merge, time and space dissolve, a single moment becomes forever.

Wolruff grips the back of my head and kisses me harder. His beard is rough against my skin, his fingers knotted tight in my hair. My sex burns for him beneath my skirts, and I part my legs and straddle him, gasping when I feel the swell of his manhood big as a mountain.

He groans as my wet undergarments press against his peak, and with a grunt his rips my tunic open. My breasts spill over my bodice, and he snaps the straps like threads and grasps my globes tight and hard. He squeezes and I arch my head back and scream, and then Wolruff's face is between my breasts and he licks me and bites me and rubs his beard all over my nipples until they rise red and hard like peaks. He sucks each nipple, taking his time with each, his big hands sliding under my skirts and grasping my thick thighs firmly. He moves me over his manhood, and I ride him as my throat tightens from an ecstasy that takes me beyond myself. My small-clothes are wet and warm, and I drip down my inner thighs as Wolruff devours my nipples and bucks his powerful hips up into me.

"By the goddess herself," I mutter as my ecstasy swells and rises and then overflows in a climax that makes my eyes roll up and my head go limp. My shoulders hunch and I convulse like a witch at the stake as the passion burns from my secret place that is hot like fire, wet like the rain. "What do you do to me, Wolruff?"

Wolruff responds by tearing off the shreds of my tunic and bodice, and then he sits up and lifts me by the waist like I am but a doll. He holds me firm and stands me up, and I look down with glazed eyes as the Viking presses his face against the front of my skirts and breathes deep of my feminine.

He groans and shudders as my scent invades him, and I see his manhood rise like a sea-serpent beneath his leather battle-dress. With one hand he pulls open his thick belt. Then he goes up on his knees and takes off his garment.

Wolruff is long as the night, thick as a log, heavy and hard and magnificent. His shaft gleams like sunfire, the head shines like a blood-moon, his clean oil oozes like sap from a swollen tree. I feel my cunt tighten and release its own wetness. Wolruff groans again like he smells my sex opening for him, and he reaches up and grasps my skirts at the waist and pulls them off me so swift my hair blows back.

I blush as the breeze from the open window blows cool against my wet thighs, but I do not think I can stay cool long. Sure enough, when Wolruff rips my small-clothes off my hips and buries his beard in my bush, the heat consumes me and I collapse onto his broad shoulders as his thick tongue snakes up my cunt and brings forth another peak that bursts like a fruit opening up in spring.

My juices pour onto his face as I scream and thrash and grab his hair just to stop myself from falling over. Wolruff grasps my buttocks and spreads them as he licks me, and when I feel his thick fingers against my dark rear hole, I gurgle and gasp and climax again like a goddess-whore, anointing the Viking with my womanly waters.

"You are a goddess," he mutters from my muff, and I shudder and smile and start to speak but stop when he taps my forbidden rear hole and then pushes a finger inside my behind. I buck forward into his face, forcing his tongue higher up my cunt. I am penetrated from front and behind, plugged good and tight with his thick tongue and fat finger. He moves his face back and forth, and I spurt again as my climax almost chokes me.

Now Wolruff pulls away, panting for air. His lips

glisten with my juices, his beard is savage and matted, his green eyes wild like a wolf's. He wipes his mouth and then rises to his feet, his hand fisting his shaft as he stares me up and down. I stand naked like a newborn, but I am without shame and without doubt. I am his and he is mine.

"I will take you now, Wendra," he says softly but with a stern authority that makes my sex clench like it has a mind of its own. I nod and he steps forth and kisses my lips. His standing cock presses firm against my mound, and I reach down with trembling hands and caress him from below.

His big body tightens and his green eyes roll up at my touch. I stroke his shaft tenderly, with long, careful strokes that give me as much pleasure as it does him. Then I reach below and hold his warm balls. They are heavy like sandbags on my palm, and I massage them and close my eyes and smile. He is full of seed and I feel my sex sigh, feel my womb whimper, feel the woman in me yearn for the man in him. In this moment I understand why the gods and goddesses play these games with their human puppets, and I know that right now they envy us, yearn for the filth of the flesh, the beauty of the blood.

The blood throbs my nether lips as Wolruff guides himself to my opening. My dark curls bristle as his head pushes through my forest, and when I feel my slit spread by his entry, opened by his advance, filled by his girth, the tears roll from my eyes like raindrops from the clouds.

Slowly Wolruff enters me, penetrating my virgin hole with care but no hesitation. Gently he pushes me back until I am firm against the cool stone wall, and then he forcefully completes the entry and flexes inside me. He holds himself there and looks upon my face. He kisses my lips, kisses me again. He slides his hands down along my curves, over my hips, around to my rump. Then suddenly he grasps my buttocks and raises me up high.

I wrap my legs around him and he brings me down onto his erect manhood, driving it so deep I feel it in my throat. I am open wide like the breached hull of a ship, and he raises me effortlessly and brings me back down while pumping upwards.

At first the force almost breaks me, and I scream and dig my nails into his broad back as the best sort of pain rips through me. But the pleasure that follows makes me lick my lips and brace for more, and when more comes I take it like a goddess.

Wolruff pumps harder now, bending his knees and bouncing me on his cock like I am a little girl. But I am no girl. I am a woman, and I lean my head back and moan without shame, howl without hesitation, scream without stopping. The Viking roars as his cock pounds into me. It gets bigger with each stroke, harder with each thrust, and soon my inner walls are stretched so wide I have to open my mouth in sympathy.

Wolruff rams me harder now, raising me and slamming me back onto his cockhead. My teeth rattle and my vision blurs, my ears ring and my body hums. My climax comes on and on like the surf crashing against the rocks, and when I feel Wolruff's heavy balls slap against my wet undersides, I sink my nails into his back and my heels into his waist and my teeth into his shoulder as I prepare to be claimed with his savage seed, pillaged by his invading heat, plundered by his raging horde.

He slams me against the wall and holds my scarred neck, pumping hard into me and then holding firm and flexing. His eyes go wide and then roll up and show me their whites. I gasp as time slows down, like the moment before a tidal wave crashes. The roar of his climax starts low in his throat, like a deep ocean swell that cannot be heard or seen but can be felt in your bones.

And I feel it not just in my bones but in my heart and my head and my fingers and my toes. I feel it everywhere, like I've felt it forever, and when it comes I am ready for it.

At least I thought I was ready.

12

WOLRUFF

Nothing in my life has readied me for the grip of pleasure so raw as this. Wendra's cunt is warm like a cradle, soft like a blanket, wet like a bath. Entering her was sublime, an experience better than pillaging and plundering, sailing into uncharted waters, leading men into battle and out in victory.

With each thrust I sink deeper into her soul, let her deeper into my heart, claim her more completely than seems possible. If the gods still watch then they are muted and mystified, silenced and stupefied. I grin and lick her face as my hips pound up into her, and when I feel my balls tighten in preparation to flood her, I pant and pump and ram hard and deep. When it comes I know it will destroy both of us, and I feel the roar of my climax building deep in my gut, ascending steadily from silence into sound.

The roar comes with an agony so beautiful I am almost broken, and I erupt in slow motion, my balls seizing up and delivering a volcanic load that makes her rise with its force. She screams and her nails rip the skin on my back, her sex pours down my shaft, her eyes roll back in her head as she flails and thrashes in my grip. My buttocks flex and hold deep inside as I shudder my way through a climax that is a lifetime in the making, an explosion with enough power to create a million new worlds, destroy a million old ones.

The roar continues with the fury of a lion, and the walls tremble as our bodies seize up. I feel her climax rip through her like windblown rain, and I shoot more of my seed into her depths, pumping and squeezing and pumping again until she overflows down my shaft and balls, our combined juices dripping heavy onto the stone floor.

I pant and drool against her neck, and my cock throbs inside her. I am still hard and big inside her, my arousal still fierce like a storm-front.

"I want you again," I growl against her skin. My

cock throbs inside her as she nods like she is not certain what I mean and does not care to be certain. I smile and pull out, holding her until her feet find the floor. She sways and swoons, and I catch her just before she falls. She smiles like an angel, giggles like a girl. Then she whispers like a woman.

"Then take me again," comes the whisper from my Wendra. "Vanquish me, you filthy Viking."

She blushes and I laugh, her playful words filling me with a joy that is the manifestation of a love so profound it threatens to overwhelm. I laugh again and lower her to the floor. She sits cross-legged and naked, her bush dark and beautiful, her scent raw and heavy. I pinch her hanging breasts and kiss her full on the mouth, and now my smile goes stiff and her giggles are gone and I feel our arousal rising up like dark smoke on a moonless night. My cock throbs and drips, and I suck her nipples and then push her down on her back.

"Turn," I say, grasping her hips and turning her. I raise her rump and stare at her magnificent globes. Slowly I spread those cheeks and look upon her dark rear hole. It shines like the moon, and I lick my lips and spit on it. She gasps and I grin, bringing my face close and licking her rim until her buttocks shudder. My arousal rises even more, and I pull back and spank her shivering buttocks hard and swift, twice on each cheek with the flat of my hand. She yelps and turns her head sideways, her eyes wide, mouth open. I grin and rub her reddening rear, then I smack her again and once again.

She screams and tries to kick at me, but I push her legs back and then jam my face down between her cheeks. At the same time I slide three fingers up her cunt from below, and suddenly she goes still as I lick her rear hole and finger her furiously.

She squirts all over my hand like a hot-spring, and I roar with delight and then rise to my knees. My cocks slaps down against her rear crease, and I spread her cheeks and press against her pucker. She gasps and hunches over, raising her rear for me. With three fingers still in her sex, I push myself into her arse. Her tight pucker resists at first but then opens for me, and she groans and whimpers as I slide into her, my shaft spreading her shiny rear canal wide open as I sail my longship into her creek.

Wendra shrieks and thrashes, and the motion explodes me with a suddenness that makes me shout and slam my palms down on her hips and push in as I fill her. My balls tighten as my chest expands. My arms flex and my buttocks clench. Again I pump my seed into Wendra, and when I see her overflow from her slit and her arse like she pays tribute to my power, I roar and shout and finally collapse upon her like I just won the prize of a lifetime, the battle of forever.

We lie together with the peace of forever, the silence of death, the quiet of eternity. Then she shifts under me and groans. I kiss her neck and chew on her thick hair. She giggles and moves her head to the side. Her big brown eyes are moist and blood-shot, wild with the madness of the night. I feel her breathe heavy, and I roll off her and pull her against my body. She burrows into me and then glares up at my face.

"So the rumors about what the Vikings do to women are true," she whispers, her eyes shining with mischief even as her cheeks bloom red and bashful.

I grunt and then grin. "Viking men are wanderers, seekers, conquerors. We lust for the uncharted territory, squeeze our longships through the narrowest of passages, seek the most elusive of entrances."

"By the goddess, the filth runs in your words just like it does in your blood," she says, smacking my arm and resting her smiling face against my chest. "I fear for the monstrous child our union will beget."

"If the child is monstrous, I will eat it and we shall have another," I say, kissing her hair gently and grinning as she smacks me again, this time harder. "What?" I say through a chuckle. "Is that not a rumor about Viking men? That we eat babies because it makes our hair grow thick and long?"

Wendra laughs against my chest, and I pet her hair and smile up at the ceiling. I glance down past my toes towards the door. Smoke still comes through the sides of the door, but the building is hard stone and now that the wood stairs are burned away, the flames are low and will not rise up.

"We are safe from the fire," I say as Wendra glances towards the door and then exhales. She looks past me towards the window, and I sigh and groan as I feel us being pulled back to the real world, away from the realm of the beautifully impossible and the magically unreasonable and the wonderfully insane.

"Wonderful," Wendra says, her gaze following mine to the open window and then back. We look at one another and then burst into laughter at the same time. Wendra smacks my chest one last time and then sits up.

I watch as she clambers to her feet and pads barefoot to her small single bed. Her bare bottom moves like a dream, and her hourglass shape makes my cock perk up even though I have discharged more seed than all the volcanoes of the North Countries put together.

Wendra leans forward, and I groan at the sight of her raised rump and the dark space between her legs. She pulls off the bedclothes and drags them off the bed. Then she glides to a small wooden shelf near the bed and unfolds another set of sheets.

"These should be long enough," she stays, frowning at the sheets and then touching the back of her head. She bites her lip and pats her round belly. Then she glances at my heavy muscle and chuckles and shakes her head. "Will it be strong enough, though?"

Now I get to my feet and look out the window. I lean over and gauge the distance. She is right. The sheets tied together will be long enough. As for strong enough . . . well, they will be strong enough for her. That is good enough.

"They will hold you," I say. "Once you are down, head to the riverbank and find one of my men. They will bring a rope that is strong enough to hold a dozen ox." As I speak, I hear a rise in the sounds of battle near the Tower. That is not a good sign. It means King Nordwin has been driven back into the streets. Soon he will be forced to retreat to the ships. She needs to hurry. Ordinarily my men would not leave without me, but I cannot forget that they are no longer my men. They serve King Nordwin now, and if the fleet is ordered to retreat, they will have no choice. "Come. Quick now. While this street is still empty and my ship is still alongside. Hurry now, Wendra. Our story is not yet complete. Our forever is not yet won. And that means the gods and goddesses are not yet done with their tricks."

13
WENDRA

Do my eyes trick me?" comes the voice just as I lower myself to the street and let go of the sheets and smooth out my skirts. I frown and look around but it is dark. The street was clear when I started my descent and it appears clear still. I look up to the window but Wolruff has ducked back inside. Perhaps he is dressing himself after making sure I got down safely. He expects me to be making haste towards the riverbank and his men. And that is what I should do.

"Yes, it is certainly a trick of the eyes or perhaps of the mind," comes the voice again, and this time I stop and squint in its direction. There is movement in the shadows across the street, in the narrow alley between two deserted buildings. They are men. Soldiers. I cannot tell which side, but I remind myself that I will be safe either way. English soldiers will not harm an Englishwoman. And if they are Vikings, then all the better! I will call out to Wolruff and he will greet them with a guffaw and a grin. So easy, I think as I force a smile and wait for the men to reveal themselves. See, Wolruff, I think. No tricks from the gods. If anything, they are now helping us get to our ending, find our forever, seize our destiny!

"Seize her," comes the voice, and finally he steps into the light and I step back when I see who it is.

King Nordwin. His crown is missing but it is him. Slightly bruised and a little bloodied, his armor hanging lopsided, his Royal Guard nursing various injuries from head to limbs. They must have fled the siege of the Tower and, being cut off from the river, were forced down the side streets. I glance up at the window. Wolruff has not seen them yet, but before I can call out the Royal Guards grab me and bring me before King Nordwin—who, to my surprise, *does* look a bit taller than I remember.

"What kind of witch are you, Mermaid?" Nordwin rasps as he leans forward but does not come closer. "You grant me one wish and not the others? You promised I would sit upon the Throne of England, but instead I am chased like a rat, defeated like a dog."

"Well, at least you are still tall," I say, offering a shrug. I speak loud and clear, and I know Wolruff must have heard us by now. What will he do, though? His ax lies broken on the street. I did not see his dagger with his battle-garments. He has no arrow to shoot. No spear to hurl.

The King licks his lips and grins. He shakes his head and shakes it again. "Yes, I am still tall," he says. Then he loses the grin and narrows his eyes at me. He sees the scar on my neck and frowns. "You were cut by the Viking, but you are still alive. Perhaps that is why only one wish came true. Perhaps two more cuts will grant me two more wishes. Yes," he whispers, licking his lips again and grinning again. "One more cut and I will sit upon the Throne of England. Then the final cut, deep and true, and I live forever." He glances at his guards. "Do it," he says. "Bleed the witch or mermaid or sorceress. Bleed her dry and make my wishes come true."

I stagger back as the guards approach, looking up at the window frantically. I do not see Wolruff, and I almost black out when I do not understand why he has not heard, why he does not throw something or at least shout! Have the gods played the ultimate trick and struck him dead? Have they given us one taste of forever and then snatched it away? Is there no end to—

And then my mind goes still and my eyes go wide and I watch in stunned silence and awed amusement as a naked cannonball of Viking muscle launches from my open window.

It is Wolruff.

Arms spread wide like wings.

Back straight and hard like it was never twisted.

Eyes green and deadly like the flying sea-monster he is.

Instead of throwing my tea-kettle or my footstool he throws himself.

Instead of shouting from above he comes down here to speak his truths.

To stake his claim.

Fight for his forever.

Destroy for his destiny.

14
<u>WOLRUFF</u>

I destroy him with my arse, landing square on King Nordwin's head and cracking his neck clean and straight. I feel his head getting pushed down into his body, and my bulk crushes him dead like an egg.

I sit there on the dead King for a moment, blinking several times as the shock of the impact recoils through my muscles and bones. But I am not hurt, and I glance down at the squished King Nordwin beneath my bare balls and naked arse and shrug.

"Well, so much for being taller," I say to the stunned Royal Guards who stand there gaping like goldfish. "It was not meant to last." Then I think a moment, raise an eyebrow, and snap my fingers at

Wendra from my perch on the King's broken body. "Ah, I see now. It is because you are no longer free, Wendra! The moment I claimed you as mine, you became my conquest, my prize, my bounty. So naturally the wishes got undone, reversed. Yes. I believe the gods and goddesses would agree."

Wendra looks at me like I am mad, and she rolls her eyes and sighs. But I am serious as a storm, and I stand and stride to Wendra, slide my arm around her waist, and dip her low and clean. I lean in and kiss her deep, smiling as I hear the gods applaud and the goddesses sigh. I kiss her once more and straighten her. She giggles and clears her throat and touches her hair, and now we turn and face the Royal Guards who know not what to do.

"Leave the King," I say sternly to the gaping guards. "He died valiantly in battle. When the English find him, they will bury him with honor. That is a better fate than he deserves. Go. Now. Forget what you saw here. It did not happen." They stare at me and shift on their feet. I smile and place my fists on my naked haunches. I feel invincible like a god, and it occurs to me that the Royal Guards just saw me fall from the heavens like a naked projectile launched by Loki the God of Mischief. They are bleeding and disoriented, and they will not engage a naked madman with fists bigger than their heads. I stand firm and stare them down, and they slowly back away from me and then turn and start to run.

Wendra laughs, and I put my arm around her. We watch as the Royal Guards fade into the backdrop, and I kiss my woman again as the stars smile down on us like they've been watching.

Watching fate play its game.

Watching destiny deal its tricks.

Watching love take its course.

A course that may twist like the tides and turn like the wind . . .

But will always lead the lovers home.

Home to their always.

Home to their forever.

∞

EPILOGUE
FIVE YEARS LATER
WENDRA

"**O**ur forever started here," I say to our four year old triplet boys Wain, Woad, and Ween. They stand with Wolruff because my arms cradle our new-born twin girls Wren and Wicca. The stout little boys are dressed in chain-mail Viking armor, and I smile at their earnest young faces. We raised them in the North Country as Vikings, but we taught them more than what the other Vikings teach their young.

We taught them that the gods and goddesses are tricksters and troublemakers, but that one must never lose faith in their fate, never be dismayed about what their destiny seems to hold. And now we made this trip on our longship to show them how twisted the path to forever can be.

"When I stood here five years ago, your father had come not to woo me but to lay waste to my land and people," I say as I stand with my Viking family and gaze upon the site of my old village. My people never returned here, and the wilderness has reclaimed the land, recycled the ruins, renewed the energy of this place. That ritual pool still remains untouched and clear, though, and I lead my brood to it and gather them around.

I look at the reflections of smiling faces in a circle. I study the young eyes of my children. I smile at the scars of my husband. Then I look into my own eyes and sigh. The water stays still and silent, smooth like glass. I smile and nod, and then I step back and lead my family back to the ship for our next stop in London.

Wolruff loads up the boys and then takes the girls from my arms and heads to the ship. I smile up at my grinning boys, walk up the plank stairway and take my place amongst them.

And then, as Wolruff takes the wheel and the boys take the rudder and I am left alone a moment, I look at the water on the pool in the distance.

I see it, and it sees me.

I know it sees me because although there is no breeze, that pool which was smooth as glass now quivers with ripples, giggles with glee, laughs with love, jiggles with joy.

And that's all I can feel as we sail away from the past and towards the future.

Laughter and giggles, joy and jiggles, always and forever.

Always and forever.

∞

FROM THE AUTHOR

Hope that was fun for you guys!

Back to modern bad boys again as the CURVY FOR KEEPS Seriesmarches on with DISCIPLIN-ING THE DUKE!

And do try my other instalove series: DRAGON'S CURVY MATE and CURVY FOR HIM!

College romance your thing? Try my CURVY IN COLLEGE Series!

Longer books your thing? Try my 23 full-length novels: CURVES FOR SHEIKHS and CURVES FOR SHIFTERS!

And do consider joining my private list at ANNABELLEWINTERS.COM/JOIN to get five never-been-published forbidden epilogues from my SHEIKHS series.

Love,
Anna.

∞

Books by Annabelle Winters

The CURVES FOR SHEIKHS Series

Curves for the Sheikh
Flames for the Sheikh
Hostage for the Sheikh
Single for the Sheikh
Stockings for the Sheikh
Untouched for the Sheikh
Surrogate for the Sheikh
Stars for the Sheikh
Shelter for the Sheikh
Shared for the Sheikh
Assassin for the Sheikh
Privilege for the Sheikh
Ransomed for the Sheikh
Uncorked for the Sheikh
Haunted for the Sheikh
Grateful for the Sheikh
Mistletoe for the Sheikh
Fake for the Sheikh

The CURVES FOR SHIFTERS Series

Curves for the Dragon
Born for the Bear
Witch for the Wolf
Tamed for the Lion
Taken for the Tiger

The CURVY FOR HIM Series

The Teacher and the Trainer
The Librarian and the Cop
The Lawyer and the Cowboy
The Princess and the Pirate

The CEO and the Soldier
The Astronaut and the Alien
The Botanist and the Biker
The Psychic and the Senator

The CURVY FOR THE HOLIDAYS Series
Taken on Thanksgiving
Captive for Christmas
Night Before New Year's
Vampire's Curvy Valentine
Flagged on the Fourth
Home for Halloween

The CURVY FOR KEEPS Series
Given to the Groom

The DRAGON'S CURVY MATE Series
Dragon's Curvy Assistant
Dragon's Curvy Banker
Dragon's Curvy Counselor
Dragon's Curvy Doctor
Dragon's Curvy Engineer
Dragon's Curvy Firefighter
Dragon's Curvy Gambler

The CURVY IN COLLEGE Series
The Jock and the Genius
The Rockstar and the Recluse
The Dropout and the Debutante
The Player and the Princess
The Fratboy and the Feminist

WWW.ANNABELLEWINTERS.

Printed in Great Britain
by Amazon